Rory
and the
Monstersitter

Rosie Reeve

BLOOMSBURY

LONDON NEW DELHI NEW YORK SYDNEY

Rory **loved** to cook.

With a bit of help from his dad, he made **blue pancakes** for breakfast...

cheese bats for lunch...

creepy crawly
buggy snacks...

...and **hairy cakes** for tea.

One evening, Mum and Dad decided to go out for dinner.

They ordered a babysitter for the children and went to get ready.

In a little while, the doorbell rang.
Rory hurried over. An **enormous**
hairy monster stood at the door.

"Do come in," said Rory, in his
politest voice. "May I take your hat?"

THE FANGLES

The huge, hairy monster grunted.
Then he stomped into the house, turned
on the TV and slumped on to the sofa.

The children went to play outside.

THE FANGLES

Fangus and Lily collected
some sticks, while Rory
played with Baby Grub.

"Be good little monsters while we're out,"
said Mum and Dad, waving goodbye.
And they set off into the forest.

Once they were out of sight, Rory, Fangus, Lily
and Baby Grub tiptoed into the house.

They sneaked past the babysitter
and went into the kitchen.

Rory got out the **biggest** saucepan he could find.

He dragged it outside and filled it with
leaves and twigs. He added a splash of water,
a twist of pepper and a sprinkling of salt.

Baby Grub added his
own special ingredient.

Not far away, Mum and Dad were having
dinner at the Cockroach Café.
They ate soup and soufflé and slimeball spaghetti.

Then they ordered puddings and coffee
and biscuits and cheese.

But back at home, tummies were rumbling.
Supper wasn't quite ready.

"I think I've left something out," said Rory.
"Something spicy?
Something hairy?
Something...BIG?"

After dinner, Mum
and Dad strolled home
in the moonlight.

When they got back, all was quiet...

The kitchen was clean and tidy.

The twins were snoring peacefully.

Baby Grub was fast asleep.

Only Rory was still awake.

"And how was the babysitter, dear?"
asked Mum and Dad.

"YUMMY!" shouted Rory.
"Totally scrumptious!

When can we have another one?"

The next morning,
everyone was
hungry again.

"Don't worry, my dears," said Mum,
"the postman will be here soon."

"YUM!" said Rory.
"I'll get the frying pan."

For Esme, who loves
to cook ~ **RR**

Bloomsbury Publishing, London, New Delhi, New York and Sydney

First published in Great Britain in 2014 by Bloomsbury Publishing Plc
50 Bedford Square, London, WC1B 3DP

A CIP catalogue record for this book is available from the British Library

ISBN 978 1 4088 4550 9 (HB)
ISBN 978 1 4088 4551 6 (PB)

Printed in China by Leo Paper Products, Heshan, Guangdong

1 3 5 7 9 10 8 6 4 2

www.bloomsbury.com